Orpheus in the Land of the Dead

Other brilliant stories to collect:

Orpheus in the Land of the Dead

Retold by
Dennis Hamley

Illustrated by
Stuart Robertson

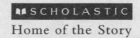

SCHOLASTIC
Home of the Story

Scholastic Children's Books,
Commonwealth House, 1–19 New Oxford Street,
London WC1A 1NU, UK
a division of Scholastic Ltd
London ~ New York ~ Toronto ~ Sydney ~ Auckland
Mexico City ~ New Delhi ~ Hong Kong

First published by Scholastic Ltd, 2001

ISBN 0 439 99612 0

Printed by Cox and Wyman Ltd, Reading, Berks.

2 4 6 8 10 9 7 5 3 1

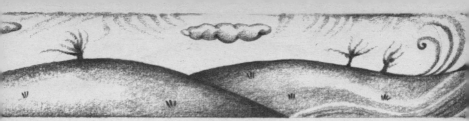

For Adam and Mary

Years ago, gods walked the earth and some humans had the blood of gods in their veins. Such a one was Orpheus. His mother was Calliope, Muse of Poetry. Some say his father was Apollo, God of the Sun. Certainly Apollo loved Orpheus enough to give him a lyre, his favourite instrument.

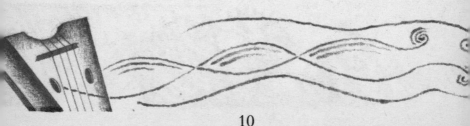

Orpheus took in every word his mother ever said until the time came when he too could make words chime in people's minds. Apollo had poured a god's power into the lyre. As soon as he could talk, Orpheus could sing and pluck the lyre's strings – and at once he could sing songs of such magic and melody that men and women, birds, beasts, fishes and even the insects were drawn towards him. They listened rapt and were never quite the same again. Humans laughed, cried and danced, savage beasts curled up like cats before the fire: even trees heard and sang their own songs to accompany him.

Orpheus grew up strong and brave. He longed for adventure and went with great heroes on some of their hardest quests – until it was time to come home to be a king in his native Thrace. Every day he sang his songs to his subjects and they loved him for it.

But Orpheus longed to marry.

There lived in Thrace a beautiful

woman whose name was Eurydice. She was nearly a goddess herself. She dwelt with the dryads and the river nymphs and seldom went near the cities of men. But one day from afar she heard Orpheus playing. She could not help herself. She walked towards the palace – and the nearer she came, the clearer and sweeter was the music. She walked faster and faster until she was running into the chamber where Orpheus played.

At once he saw her. She was slender and fair: Orpheus had never seen any woman remotely near her beauty.

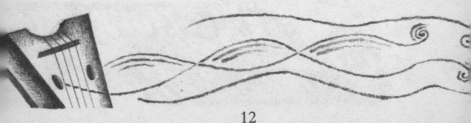

From then on, his music was for her alone.

Eurydice heard his voice, now high, now low, always pure like crystal, singing of great adventures in far-off lands. His lyre poured out melodies which seemed like gold falling drop by drop into her mind. In her eyes, Orpheus was the sun come down to earth: in her ears, he was the harmony of gods on Olympus. Long before he had finished, Eurydice was in love with him.

Orpheus felt her love wreathe him like sea waves. She was beautiful

and trusting. In return he loved her at once.

The wedding was a wonderful affair, attended by the gods themselves. Hymen, Apollo's son and the God of Marriage, was there, to bless the couple with his flaming torch. What greater omens could there be of love, happiness and fortune?

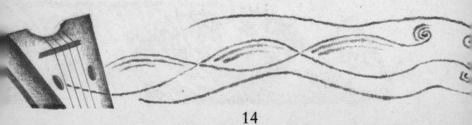

There was music and dancing and a great feast. Delight and content flooded through every guest. Soon it was time for Hymen to light his torch and bless Orpheus and Eurydice.

Everyone waited. Orpheus and Eurydice stood, hand in hand, to receive this final proof that the gods smiled on their marriage. But when Hymen lit the flame, instead of a bright, steady blaze. . .

Black smoke swirled everywhere. The guests coughed and choked. Orpheus's eyes stung and watered. "What's happening?" cried Eurydice.

"The gods are angry. We're not meant to marry."

But Orpheus held her close. "Of course we are," he said. "If we keep vigilant and faithful, then all will be well."

So the wedding feast ended and the guests went home sad and worried for them both. Orpheus and Eurydice were on their own and resolved to be loyal to each other and watchful of the world.

But there are some things which, it seems, no amount of watchfulness and loyalty can prevent.

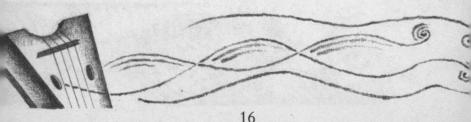

Deep in the country lived a man called Aristos. He was steeped in country crafts: some say he was a god of the countryside. But if he was a god, he was not like Apollo or Jupiter. He was sullen, cunning and crafty. He lived alone, deep in the forest, and shunned the rest of the world.

What he was best at was bee-

keeping: it was he who first understood how to make these wild insects give up their honey. He set up his hives in the beautiful valley of the River Peneus — on his own, to keep his honey for himself. If he had his way, nobody else would share it, or find out how to tame the wild bees.

He did not know that Orpheus and Eurydice lived nearby in perfect happiness, or that Eurydice sometimes walked here with her friends the river nymphs. Nor did Eurydice and Orpheus know what lurked so close in the forest.

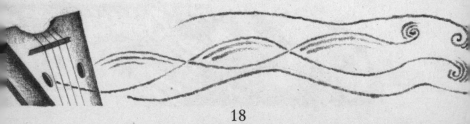

One day, Eurydice and her nymphs were walking by the river. From behind a tree, Aristos saw them. Or rather, he saw Eurydice. At once, he wanted her for himself. He tore off his bee-keeper's smock and veil and ran towards her.

Eurydice saw only a hairy creature with a leering, creased, evil face.

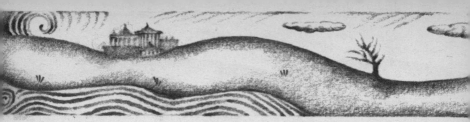

The nymphs scattered and disappeared into the water: she was on her own, facing something out of a bad dream. She ran for her life. Aristos ran too, chasing Eurydice, coming ever nearer and nearer...

In her panic she did not look where she was going. She never saw a snake lying peaceably in the grass, sunning itself. She trod on it, and the snake, as snakes will, immediately struck. Its fangs sank deep into her foot: soon poison flooded her body and she lay dead on the bank of the River Peneus.

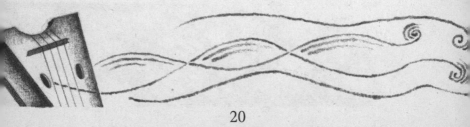

Aristos stopped. Then he hid among the trees because he knew what would happen to him when Eurydice was found. Thus he escaped the revenge of Orpheus. But the gods were angry with him. He came back to his hives to find all his bees were gone, the fruits and berries he ate were shrivelled and dead and the forest did not

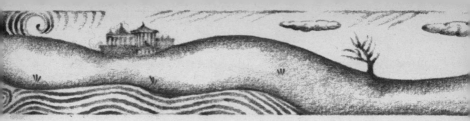

want to know him any more. Long and hard was the lonely penance the gods now made him go through.

When Eurydice's body was brought to Orpheus, he was grief-stricken. Even when she was about to be buried, he refused to believe she was dead. "I see her body in the ground," he cried. "But I know that somewhere she's still alive and waiting for me. I won't rest

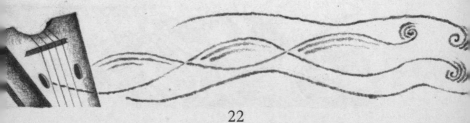

until I find her." He placed a coin under her tongue to pay the fare to Charon the ferryman, who would take her across the River Styx when she reached the Underworld. Then he vowed that, somehow or other, he would visit the Underworld himself and bring her back.

"But nobody still alive has ever been to that awful place and come back to tell us," cried his friends.

"Hercules has," Orpheus replied. "So has Theseus. They are great heroes and also my friends. Where they went, I'll follow. All the while I

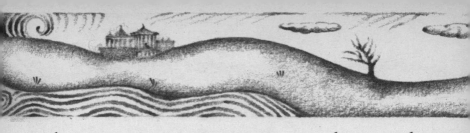

have my music, I can go anywhere and do anything."

When he said that, his people were sadder than ever. Still, they could see how terrible his grief was. If he was determined to die as well, there was nothing anyone could do to stop him.

So Orpheus set out, with nothing but his lyre and his songs, to look for an entrance to the Underworld. He knew

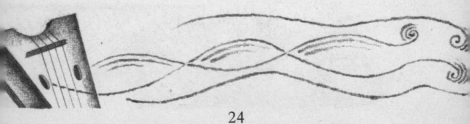

that somewhere in Thrace there was a way in. "Look for a place where no birds sing," people said. Far into the barren wastes he went, eating the few berries and roots that he found, sleeping under the stars with only rocks for shelter. Wild animals threatened him: he charmed them with his music. Winds and storms rose up: he stilled them with his songs.

For years he searched. By now he was thin and as wiry as the animals. His skin was burnt brown by the sun and toughened by winds and rain. Other men would have forgotten

Eurydice, come home and married again. Not Orpheus. His love was steadfast and he would never give up.

One day he reached a dry, shrivelled-up sort of place which echoed with its own silence. There were no birds in the sky, no creatures on the ground except for a few bleached skeletons. He found a dark opening in the side of a mountain, like the entrance to a cave.

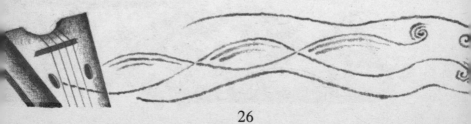

A strange, choking smoke, worse by far than that from Hymen's torch, swirled out. "A birdless place," he said. "Have I reached the Underworld at last?"

He entered. The bright light of day disappeared behind him. He was in a narrow passage which sloped steeply downwards. The tunnel was slippery and falling stones clattered round him. The dark was complete and a foul smell grew stronger the further down he felt his way.

At last he heard water lapping in front of him. He staggered on. Light grew slightly: a strange, unearthly

glow. He was by a river: he knew it for the River Styx. Across the other side were Hades and Persephone, King and Queen of the Underworld. It was them he had to persuade to let Eurydice leave. But there were still fearsome obstacles. As he stood hesitating, there grew a ghastly groaning so terrible as to chill his very soul. He was surrounded by flitting grey shapes which touched his face with cold spectral fingers that would suffocate him. The ghosts of the dead, he thought. They will stop me, a living man, from entering.

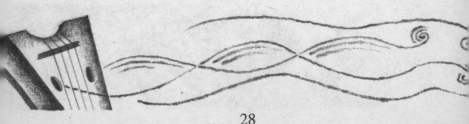

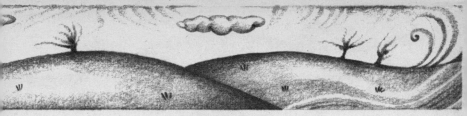

What could he do? He took his lyre from his back and started to sing and play. Such a wondrous sound had never been heard before beside the River Styx. The ghosts fell back, screaming with amazement at such beauty in this place.

What next? Orpheus could make out the shape of a boat far across the river. It was coming nearer. Now he could

see the hooded skeletal figure poling it along. Charon, the ferryman, treacherous and grasping, ancient and withered yet strong like a bull.

The boat scrunched up on the pebbly shore. Orpheus saw sunken, glittering eyes under the ferryman's hood. "My fare," said Charon. "Pay me my fare before you come aboard."

For answer, Orpheus plucked the strings of his lyre and his voice soared upwards in the loveliest melody he could think of. Charon listened, rapt. Then, without another word, he motioned Orpheus on board. For a long

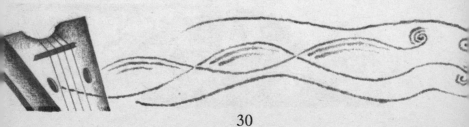

time there was no sound but Charon's
wheezy gasping as he poled his boat,
the slap of water and an ominous
gurgling as more water seeped through
the rotting, leaky timbers.

The voyage seemed to take for ever.
But it ended at last and Orpheus
stepped out on to the other shore.
Charon leant on his pole and laughed
without mirth. "Much good may your

crossing do you," he said.

How right he seemed to be. At once, Orpheus faced another hazard. An unearthly roar deafened him: a giant, fearsome creature barred his way. It was a huge, slavering, sharp toothed, three-headed dog, with stinging serpent tails: Cerberus, set to guard the opposite bank of the Styx against all who should not be there.

Now what could Orpheus do? His music had tamed savage animals on the surface of the earth well enough, but this supernatural beast was a different matter. The monstrous dog reared up. His tails swished and the deadly stings missed Orpheus by a fingertip's width as he swayed backwards. One of Cerberus's thick necks thrust forward. The first mighty mouth opened wide, then clamped shut so the teeth jarred together with a grinding thump. But Orpheus had darted out of the way like the most nimble of wrestlers.

Cerberus gathered himself for another strike — but Orpheus was ready. He plucked the first notes on his lyre and sang the song that had calmed lions and wolves in the desert. Cerberus blinked with all six eyes, listened with six ears — then one mouth yawned, the next barked softly and the third whined with a strange pleasure.

The vast dog stretched itself out. Its tails thumped on the ground and it rolled over to show its monstrous stomach as if it wanted Orpheus to tickle it.

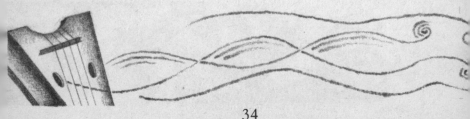

But Orpheus only wanted to get past the monster, not make friends with it. He still had a long way to go. On he went, past the moaning spirits of the damned, past Tantalus doomed never to reach the fruit on the bough, Sisyphus forced always to push a boulder uphill but fated never to see it reach the top, the daughters of Danaos trying to empty a lake with

sieves, all the other poor spirits sentenced to eternal punishments.

He never stopped playing his music: soon it reached every corner of the Underworld. The damned souls stopped their futile eternal tasks. Tantalus stopped reaching for the grapes which would never be his. Sisyphus sat resting on his boulder. The daughters of Danaos put down their sieves. For everyone there was just an instant of happiness. All ears kept listening, hoping this sudden, unexpected beauty would last for ever.

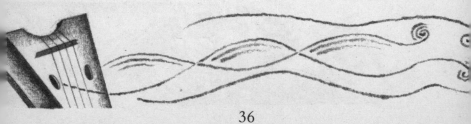

At last, the journey was over. Orpheus entered the royal palace of the Underworld. In front of him were the thrones of Hades and Persephone. The severe faces of the ruler and his wife glared down on him. Flanking them were the sinister judges of the newly dead. Awestruck, Orpheus stopped playing and lowered his lyre.

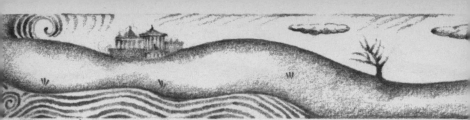

Hades spoke. "No," he said. "Play. I want to hear for myself this sound which seems to enchant every spirit in the Underworld. When I'm satisfied, you can tell me what extraordinary errand brings a living man here."

So Orpheus played again, for hours and hours, every song that he could remember. The faces of Hades and Persephone softened. Even the judges

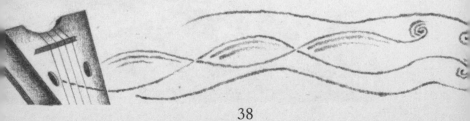

relaxed and looked almost happy. At last, Hades raised his hand.

"That's enough," he said. "Now, tell us what you want."

Orpheus knelt. His heart was beating fast: every word he said was going to matter now.

"Hades and Persephone, I know that everyone alive has to come before this throne in the end. I also know that my time has not come yet. Please believe I'm not here to find out the secrets of the Underworld so that living men can conquer it. I'm not trying to make it easy for dead men

39

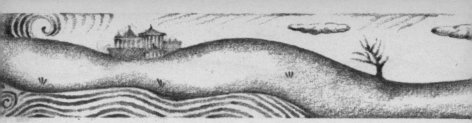

either: I've not come to drown Charon or kill Cerberus. No, I've come to release someone else whose time should not have come yet but is here nevertheless."

"Tell me more," said Hades. "I never knew there could be a ghost down here whose time had not yet come."

"My lord, I mean my dear wife Eurydice," Orpheus replied. "She was young, she was beautiful and we loved each other. She should have died in the fulness of her years. But she was struck down by a venomous snake and

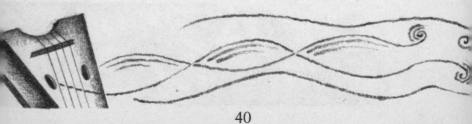

her soul was taken away. I don't believe her true time had come and I don't believe you would either if you knew her."

"Orpheus," said Hades. "Many come here young, killed in war or dead through disease or accident. Who is to say that they deserved what happened to them? But remember – we are deep under the ground here. Anyone who reaches the surface again does so not as a human but as a plant, a tree, a flower. I have no power to alter that."

He stopped. Persephone spoke. "Listen," she said.

There was silence all through the Underworld. Every spirit was listening, hoping that the wonderful music would start again. Hades was silent and thoughtful: then he looked at Orpheus with new eyes.

"Very well," he said. "You've brought a power to the Underworld beyond what I thought any mortal man had. So you may have Eurydice back."

But before Orpheus could cry with joy and stammer out his thanks, Hades went on. "There is a condition," he said.

"What is it?" asked Orpheus. "Say anything you want and I'll do it."

"Eurydice, come here," Hades called. At once, she was there, pale and ghostly — but without doubt his own wife.

"Now you know she is here and this is no trick," said Hades. "My condition is this. You will go back exactly the way you came. You won't deviate from your track by so much as a hand's-width. You must take it

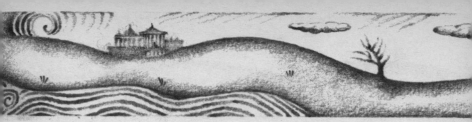

on trust that she is there. You will never look round to make sure she is following. If you so much as take a single split-second glance at her before you reach the world above us, she will vanish and you'll lose her for ever. But if you can do as I say, then she'll be with you to live out the whole of her natural life. Is that fair?"

"Very fair, great King Hades," Orpheus replied.

"Then go – and once you've left the Underworld all the eternal tortures will start again, for you'll never return until you're dead yourself."

So Orpheus took one last long look at
Eurydice before he had to turn away.
Then he set off, leaving Hades,
Persephone and the judges like grim
statues watching after him. He felt
uneasy. He wondered if he had been
somehow tricked or whether a terrible
disaster would happen on the way out.
Would Cerberus wake up? Would
Charon refuse to take a spirit *and* a

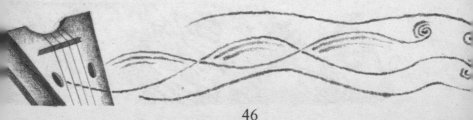

living man back across the river? He passed the ghosts of the damned, all watching him with longing for the music he was taking away. He passed Cerberus, who growled in his sleep, then stirred and opened one eye on each head. He came to Charon, who could not remember the last time his boat was occupied for the return journey. "I will not take you," said the ancient ferryman. "Hades would forbid it."

"Hades commands you," Orpheus replied. "Can't you see you have a second passenger?"

Charon looked at him strangely —
a look which caused a flicker of doubt
in Orpheus's mind. Nevertheless, he
stood in the bows of the boat, looked
straight ahead and refused to believe
that Hades would cheat him.

Charon poled his craft across and never
asked for a fare. Orpheus stepped out
on the other side and the pale ghosts
parted and let him through.

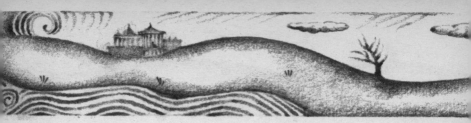

Now he had reached the long passage which emerged at the birdless place in the deserts of Thrace. It stretched steeply upwards into pitch darkness. He stood facing the long ascent. He listened. There was no sound behind him.

He set off again. Immediately, he heard other footsteps. Were they just an echo of his own? Or were they Eurydice's. Had Cerberus woken and followed him, padding on huge feet, with three wicked mouths slavering? Or had Charon left his boat to tread purposefully behind, eyes burning in

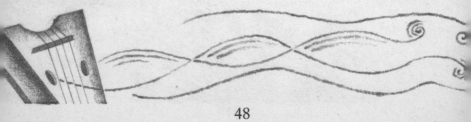

that skull of a face? Was he followed by something else that was sinister and deadly?

He had to take everything on trust – that was the bargain. So he set out, resolutely looking in front of him.

The toil upwards was long and hard. His feet kept dislodging stones which clattered away behind him. Could he still hear footsteps? Were they made by Eurydice? Did none of the stones hit her as they fell past? If they did, why wasn't she crying out with pain?

He stopped again. The last few dislodged stones fell to rest: then there was silence, complete and profound. Perhaps Eurydice had lost sight of him in the dark. Perhaps she had left the track and now blundered blindly round winding passages with no end.

He had to guide her back to him. He took his lyre from off his back and played, quietly at first, then louder. He sang their favourite songs.

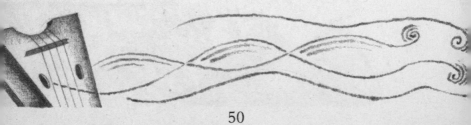

When she heard them she would know which way to go.

At last he stopped singing. Again he listened. Once the echoes of his music had died away, there was again the same frightening silence.

Hopelessly, he walked on. His panic grew. The temptation to steal just the merest glance back was almost overpowering. He was on the

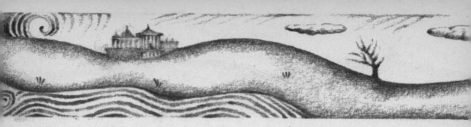

point of doing it. But then he heard Hades's voice: "She will vanish and you'll lose her for ever."

That voice echoed over and over again in his ears. For hours he toiled on upwards, ears straining for the slightest sound behind him. Now his resolve not to look back was iron-hard and never wavered.

At last there was light ahead. They were near the surface. He stopped for the last time. Did he hear her now? Yes, surely that slight rustle was from her. No, he'd imagined it. How could that be? There was only one answer. Hades had tricked him. She wasn't there after all.

Daylight through the tunnel entrance was clear on him. Another few paces and he would be out. He heard Hades's voice again: "Once you're out of the Underworld all the eternal tortures will begin again, for you'll never return until you're dead yourself."

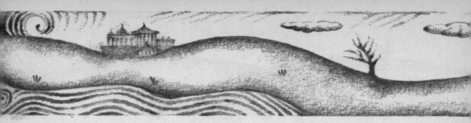

But if that was true, then once he was outside and she was not with him he would have lost her for ever.

He could not bear it another second. He had to look, to be sure, to be ready to run back into the Underworld and find her again.

So he turned. And in that instant he saw her there, coming out of the tunnel, sunlight on her face, smiling with joy, arms outstretched towards him. But even as he looked, the foul smoke which shrouded the entrance fell again. She disappeared from his gaze. He heard her dear voice through the fog. "Goodbye, Orpheus. We've lost each other for ever now. Remember our love, for memories are all that are left to you." The smoke lifted: the tunnel was empty. She had disappeared, and he knew she was gone for the whole of eternity. Perhaps Hades spoke true. Not even he had the power to alter how the dead could appear again on the Earth.

He stood alone, desolate, empty, too devastated even to cry. It would be a long, dismal journey back home when he was supposed to be returning in joy.

He took his lyre and started to play a melody to express his grief. But no: even music seemed to fail him now.

He drew his arm back to hurl the lyre away.

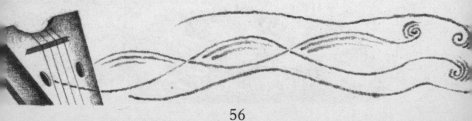

Then he stopped. No, music was little use now. But one day it might be again. And for now it was all he had left.

Head down, shoulders hunched, he started on the long, lonely trail back to his empty palace.

As Orpheus approached his palace, word spread that he was returning. People lined the streets to see him and

his rescued Eurydice. But when they saw him trail along, dragging his lyre behind him and realized he was alone, they drew back and whispered to each other, because they feared the worst for him.

Orpheus passed them all without a single look. He walked up the steps to the palace. When he reached the top, he turned and at last spoke.

"Never, for as long as I live, shall I set eyes on a woman again," he shouted.

Then he let himself inside. The door closed on him with a mighty thud.

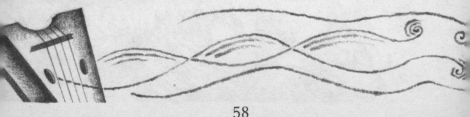

For months there was no sign of life from the palace. The people stole round it and tried to look in its windows. They listened at its doors, for some sign that Orpheus was still alive.

There was none.

Then, one day, they heard something. That familiar voice and the wonderful lyre, soft at first, then louder and louder, until the whole of

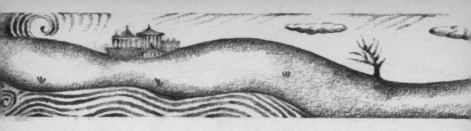

Thrace rang again with Orpheus's music.

And the people of Thrace were happy for Orpheus, because though he would never see his Eurydice again until death, at least they knew he had the other part of his life which made it worth living. And he was sharing it with them as well, which was all they wanted now.

Other stories to collect:

The Ugly Duckling

Helen Dunmore

Illustrated by Robin Bell Corfield

Once upon a time there was an ugly duckling
that didn't have a friend in the world…

The Musicians
of Bremen

Ann Jungman

Illustrated by James Marsh

Once upon a time there was a donkey
who ran away from home…

Beauty and the Beast

Tessa Krailing

Illustrated by Diana Mayo

Once upon a time there was a beautiful girl
who was forced to live with a hideous Beast...

King Herla's Ride

Jan Mark

Illustrated by Jac Jones

Once upon a time there was a king who lived
upon a hill and a king who lived under one...

The Little Mermaid

Linda Newbery

Illustrated by Bee Willey

Once upon a time there was a mermaid
who rescued a prince from drowning…

The Pedlar of
Swaffham

Philippa Pearce

Illustrated by Rosamund Fowler

Once upon a time there was a pedlar
who had an unforgettable dream…